More **Dark Man** books:

Dark Man

The Dark Dreams of Hell
by Peter Lancett
illustrated by Jan Pedroietta

Published by Ransom Publishing Ltd.
51 Southgate Street, Winchester, Hampshire SO23 9EH
www.ransom.co.uk

ISBN   978 184167 418 6
First published in 2006
Second printing 2008

A CIP catalogue record of this book is available from the British Library.

The rights of Peter Lancett to be identified as the author and of Jan Pedroietta to be identified as the illustrator of this Work have been asserted by them in accordance with sections 77 and 78 of the Copyright, Design and Patents Act 1988.

David Strachan, The Old Man, and The Shadow Masters appear by kind permission of Peter Lancett.

Printed in China through Colorcraft Ltd., Hong Kong.

Dark Man

The
Dark Dreams
of Hell

by Peter Lancett

illustrated by Jan Pedroietta

Ransom

Chapter One:
The Old Man's Home

The Dark Man is in the smart part of the city.

He is at the home of the Old Man.

The Dark Man is weary and sits back in a chair.

"How long must I live like this?" the Dark Man asks.

The Old Man thinks before he speaks.

"The Shadow Masters will never stop,"
he says.

Chapter Two:
The Dark Man's Question

"What if they did find the Golden Cup?" the Dark Man asks.

"Would it be so bad?"

"Close your eyes," the Old Man says softly.

"Sleep."

The Old Man's words have power, so the
Dark Man sleeps.

As he sleeps, he is visited by dreams.

Chapter Three:
The Dark Dreams

He sees the bad part of the city and it is in flames.

Men and women are crying out.

Some are lying dead in the streets as others burn.

Demons force others to drag a huge wagon.

On the wagon is a vast, stone, evil god.

In dark corners, looking at this world they have made, are Shadow Masters.

Then the Dark Man sees that this is not the bad part of the city.

It is the smart part!

Chapter Four:
The Dark Man's Destiny

He wakes with a scream.

The Old Man has gone.

He lets himself out onto the street.

It is night as he heads back to the bad part of the city.

Now he knows why he cannot ever rest.

The author

photograph: Rachel Ottewill

Peter Lancett used to work in the movies. Then he worked in the city. Now he writes horror stories for a living. "It beats having a proper job," he says.